Main Street, U.S.A.

Roughly three million passengers ride the Walt Disney World Railroad every year as its five narrow-gauge steam trains circumvent the Park in a clockwise direction. Constructed between 1916 and 1928, the four original Philadelphia-built trains were discovered in the Yucatán, where they were used to haul sugar and jute. Engine No. 5 was built in 1927

in Davenport, Iowa. The tunnels set underneath the trestle open on to Town Square, which bustles with an assortment of vehicles, including horse-drawn trolleys, horseless carriages, and even a fire engine that transports visitors up and down the street. Engine Co. 71 at the redbricked Fire Station draws its name from the year Walt Disney World opened.

The Emporium was "founded" in 1901 (the year Walt was born). Its Victorian décor was expanded upon recently, as the proprietor decided to add more Edwardian elements, including crown molding and stained-glass windows. The chandelier now combines the original gas lamps (pointing up) with new electric lights (pointing down).

A stroll along Main Street winds past The Harmony Barber Shop, which specializes in "first haircuts." Hair tonics and talcum powders line the dark burgundy shelves, and customers are serenaded by The Dapper Dans Barbershop Quartet throughout the day. Further on, The Hall of Champions has very "winning" apparel, and the baseball-themed Casey's Corner serves hot dogs and fries accompanied by ragtime piano music. The Crystal Palace, with its impressive glass facade, acts as a transition point between Main Street and the Colonial-style Victorian architecture seen in Adventureland.

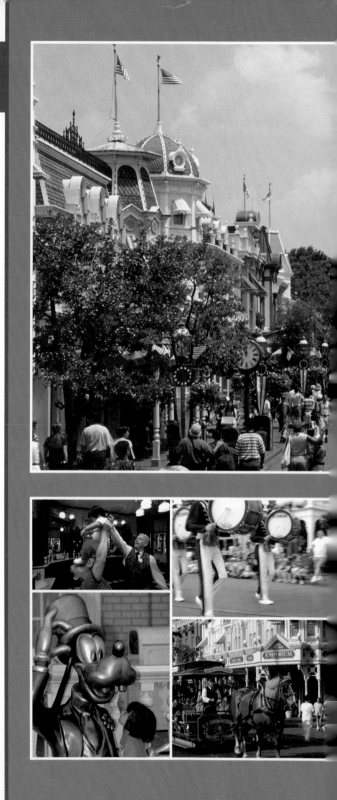

Main Street, U.S.A., depicts America at the turn of the last century during a time of burgeoning progress. It's everyone's hometown, where the smiles are as sweet as the smell of fresh cakes coming from the nearby bakery. The various "businesses," etched into the windows above the ground floors, honor the men and women who were instrumental in the construction of the Park. Walt Disney's name appears twice—once on a window above the railroad station and again near the Hub on a window facing Cinderella Castle.

The inspiration for Tony's Town Square Restaurant was the animated film *Lady and the Tramp*, and a *buono* meal of spaghetti and meatballs might be accompanied by the song "Bella Notte." Paw prints enclosed in a heart can be found in the sidewalk out front. On the other end of Town Square Exposition Hall, Goofy casts a solid shadow with a purple top hat and a red boutonniere. Main Street Confectionery features a gingerbread trim on its cupboards, and a wide selection of fudge, caramel apples, cotton candy, and peanut brittle—most of which is created right in front of you.

Uptown Jewelers, specializing in jewelry, snow globes, figurines, and timepieces, is the place to find that special Mickey Mouse watch to adorn your wrist. On the Hub, the Partners statue, dedicated on June 19, 1995, captures Walt and Mickey. Another statue honors Roy O. Disney, who relaxes with Minnie while seated on a bench on the Town Square.

Adventureland

The Enchanted Tiki Room— Under New Management

Based on the first Audio-Animatronics show ever created, The Enchanted Tiki Room—Under New Management, has some new "fowl" landlords, and not a few feathers will be ruffled before the last note is warbled. The performance begins as Jose, Michael, Fritz, and Pierre lead the revered (and repetitive) "In the Tiki Tiki Tiki Tiki Tiki Room," then Iago from *Aladdin* announces his plans for an all-new show. Zazu from *The Lion King* warns him that changes will anger the tiki gods, but Iago will not be swayed off his perch and starts his renovation with a toe-tapping, updated version of "Friend Like Me." In a blast of green vapor, the tiki goddess of disaster, Uh Oa, rises up from the center floral display and sends a bolt hurling toward Iago, who disappears in a cloud of smoke. When he returns (bandaged and on crutches) the parrot concedes that the tiki gods are the greatest act he's ever heard. The singing 88 birds and 132 flowers, 20 drum-thumping tiki gods, and 48 masks celebrate this with a number that gets everyone on their feet—and out the doors!

The Magic Carpets of Aladdin

Agrabah Bazaar bustles with merchants peddling their shiny wares. Even its streets contain bling—pieces of pottery, gems, and tile are embedded in the concrete. At the center of this oasis, magic carpets fly around a giant bottle topped by the Genie's lamp. Riders in front control the height of their flight, while backseaters use a scarab-shaped button to control the pitch. Beware—your wishes may be dampened temporarily by the spitting camels that surround you!

Jungle Cruise

Entering a colonial outpost in a remote section of the jungle, brave explorers board a canopied launch for a cruise down the tropical "rivers of the world." "Fishing is prohibited," proclaims an announcement, "unless you happen to be fishing a relative out of the water!" The guides might be a little cut-rate, but it's an exciting trip you won't soon forget (unlike some of the bad jokes that permeate the excursion).

The idea for Jungle Cruise evolved from the Academy Award–winning True-Life Adventures films. Walt originally wanted to feature live animals, but since their sleeping habits coincided with passengers' viewing habits, a new plan was forged. Five hundred varieties of plant life landscape the area to evoke a tropical feel, and the rivers contain approximately 1,750,000 gallons of water, churned up by waterfalls at each end of the journey.

Jungle Cruise first traverses the Amazon through the rain forests of Brazil, in South America, then glides over to Central Africa on the Congo. Traveling to the Nile, passengers can also see the back side of water on Schweitzer Falls, named after the great explorer, Dr. Albert . . . Falls. Be sure to smile back at the crocodiles, "Old Smiley" and his girlfriend, Ginger (she snaps). And don't worry—the hippos on the river aren't dangerous, unless they wiggle their ears! The plane seen in the African Veldt is actually only half a plane—the other half is in The Great Movie Ride at Disney's Hollywood Studios. The journey concludes on the Mekong River of Southeast Asia under the eyes of a watchful tiger that guards a golden monkey idol already protected by pythons.

Pirates of the Caribbean

Booming cannons ring out over the Castillo del Morro citadel from the Torre del Sol (Tower of the Sun) watchtower, over one of the most treasured attractions in the Park. To the surprise of many, Pirates of the Caribbean wasn't at Magic Kingdom Park upon its opening in 1971. The Park's planners assumed that since Florida was located relatively close to the Caribbean, there would be little interest in a pirate-themed experience. However, the popularity of the attraction in Disneyland won them over and the pirates invaded Adventureland in 1973.

For more than thirty years, the pirates happily plundered and looted, at first chasing the townswomen for their affection, then for their food, before getting chased themselves for their pillaging. The motion picture based upon the ride inspired an updated version in 2006 featuring Captain Barbossa in pursuit of Jack Sparrow (sorry…Captain Jack Sparrow) as he attempts to acquire a map to the town's treasure. Now, before dropping down a waterfall and sailing through ghostly grottoes strewn with skeletal scalawags, the bateaux glide through a misty waterfall where the image of Davy Jones reminds us that "Dead Men Do Tell Tales."

The boats then enter a Caribbean port under attack by the *Wicked Wench*, captained by Barbossa, who shouts, "Strike yer colors, you bloomin' cockroaches!" In town, a rowdy band of buccaneers is dunking the mayor for information as they search for Jack. But Jack finds ways not to be seen, such as hiding behind a dressmaker's dummy or inside a barrel. Voyagers pass by a boisterous bride auction, a fiery night on the town, and jail cells (where that dog *still* won't give up those keys!) to discover that the clever captain has found his treasure, as a gold-festooned Jack celebrates.

No, the two skeletons playing chess along the queue didn't forget to get a FastPass—they're deadlocked in a state of perpetual check, in which the only available move will result in a circlet of moves that can never be broken.

Frontierland

Frontierland's time line spans from roughly 1790 to 1880, recalling different eras from American folklore—from the frontier of Davy Crockett and the banks of the mighty Mississippi once traveled by Tom Sawyer to the Southwest of Pecos Bill and Big Thunder's ghost town from the post-gold rush of 1849. The address on each building of Frontierland indicates its year of construction. At Pecos Bill Tall Tale Inn and Café, the folklore hero has decorated his "waterin' hole" with mementos such as Paul Bunyan's ax, John Henry's hammer, and Annie Oakley's six-shooters.

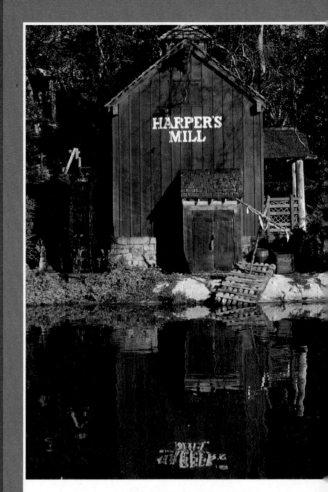

Tom Sawyer Island

Explorers who raft over to Tom Sawyer Island, based on the timeless tale by Mark Twain, will be able to follow in Tom and Huck Finn's footprints on two islands connected by a long rope bridge aptly named Superstition. Scrub pines border each trail, which lead to caves, overlooks, a floating barrel bridge, and Fort Langhorne. The strummin' of a fiddle and the plinkin' of a banjo are punctuated by the plashing of water through the wheel at Harper's Mill. Aunt Polly's Dockside Inn, which extends into the Rivers of America, is the perfect place to get a glass of lemonade and relax.

Country Bear Jamboree

A hilarious cast of wilderness bears perform in a foot-stompin' hoedown. Country Bear Jamboree is one of the few attractions that debuted in Florida before finding its way to Disneyland. The concept for Country Bear Jamboree originated in another project Walt and his Imagineers planned for a California ski resort, where the Country Bear Playhouse would feature an Audio-Animatronics musical show. The ski resort was never realized, but the Country Bears were not forgotten and found their way to Florida for the Park's premiere.

Acts include Henry, the Master of Ceremonies; the Five Bear Rugs; Liver Lips McGrowl; the Sun Bonnets (Bunny, Bubbles, and Beulah); and Teddi Barra (who descends from the ceiling of Grizzly Hall on a swinging perch). Melvin (moose), Buff (buffalo), and Max (stag) are mounted on the wall, and offer wry commentary and a solid baritone. The production has showcased new approaches through the years, including the Country Bear Christmas Special and the Country Bear Vacation Hoedown.

Big Thunder Mountain Railroad

Set during the gold rush era in the flooded mining town of Tumbleweed established in Dry Gulch, the 2.5 acre mountain that Big Thunder Mountain Railroad travels over is chock-full of gold—or so the legend goes. The town wasn't always so damp, however, suffering from a drought (Population— Dried Out!) until "Professor" Cumulus Isobar, self-claimed "Rainmaker Extraordinaire and Purveyor of Magical Elixirs," came to lend his "skills."

After arriving via Nugget Road, passengers enter the deserted headquarters of the Big Thunder Mining Co. and board converted ore cars through a deserted mine shaft. Within sight are the sun-bleached bones of a dinosaur, while geysers spurt, bubble, and erupt nearby. As the trains wind around the majestic mountain and its distinctive Spiral Butte, travelers brave flash floods, rumbling earthquakes, crashing landslides, and hairpin turns. (Perhaps that's why this is known as "The Wildest Ride in the Wilderness!")

Along the rustic Southwestern landscape, reminiscent of the brilliantly colored scenery found in Arizona's Monument Valley, the ride is punctuated by narrow gorges, tunnels, windswept caverns, and dry riverbeds, as well as donkeys, goats, chickens, and spinning opossums. The washed-up miner inhabiting the bathtub floating by during the flash flood is named Cousin Elrod. Prior to the attraction's opening, Imagineers scoured ghost towns out West to decorate it with authenticity. The genuine antique mining equipment found through the area includes a double-stamp ore crusher, an ore-hauling wagon, and an old ball mill used to extract gold.

Splash Mountain

This thrilling log-flume excursion takes its inspiration from three sequences featuring Brer Rabbit, Brer Bear, and Brer Fox from the 1946 combination animated/live-action film *Song of the South*, based on the "Uncle Remus" tales written by Joel Chandler Harris. Hollowed-out logs (carved out by sharp-toothed beavers, as the story goes) float through the twisting backwoods waterways of the flooded mountain, eventually joining up with Brer Rabbit, who is looking for some fun on the kind of day sung about in the song "Zip-A-Dee-Doo-Dah." But his archrivals, Brer Fox and Brer Bear, are scheming to catch the happy-go-lucky rabbit and put an end to his carefree rambling. Spooky caves, hollow trees, and skulking, silhouetted pursuers follow the logs before they plunge down Chickapin Hill and the world's longest flume chute (52 feet) into the Briar Patch at its base.

Splash Mountain features one of the largest groups of Audio-Animatronics figures in a Walt Disney World attraction (including the two top-hatted vultures that watch as each log begins its descent down the flume) and the largest animated prop at any Disney park in the *Zip-A-Dee Lady* showboat, which is thirty-six-feet long and twenty-two-feet high. The first plunge goes over Slippin' Falls. The final plunge takes place at an approximate 45 degree angle, descending at a speed greater than that of the rockets soaring through Space Mountain in Tomorrowland.

Liberty Square

The *Liberty Belle*

The *Liberty Belle*, an authentic steam-powered stern-wheeler, cruises the Rivers of America. The riverboat actually has a boiler room that converts the river water into steam that then powers the paddle that propels the boat. Along the journey, scenes placed on the riverbank depict an Algonquin camp and a settler's shack set in Alligator Swamp. River markers let you know when you're passing Devil's Elbow, Tree Snag Reef, and Howling Dog Bend. Watch for the mule deer wiggling their ears as you sail over Deer Crossing Shallows and listen for the sounds of raucous river pirates celebrating in Wilson's Cave Inn.

Liberty Square

There is a chrono*logical* progression of time through Liberty Square. At the entry, the architecture of Sleepy Hollow refreshments displays an early 1700s Dutch New Amsterdam river stone and wood-shingle style, which soon gives way to the 1780-ish Williamsburg-Georgian design of The Hall of Presidents. On its Fantasyland border, a New England waterfront–type atmosphere of the early 1800s prevails at the Columbia Harbour House. On the opposite side, the buildings become rougher-hewn and more reminiscent of the Northwest Territory. This progression of time continues in the styles of Frontierland's architecture.

The Liberty Tree is a Southern live oak—*querous Virginana*. It's more than one hundred years old and is the largest living thing in Magic Kingdom Park at forty feet high, sixty feet wide, and thirty-eight tons. It features thirteen hanging lanterns, symbolizing the original thirteen colonies. The nearby Liberty Bell was cast in 1989 from the same mold as the original, so it is a "second generation" of the bell. The mold was subsequently destroyed.

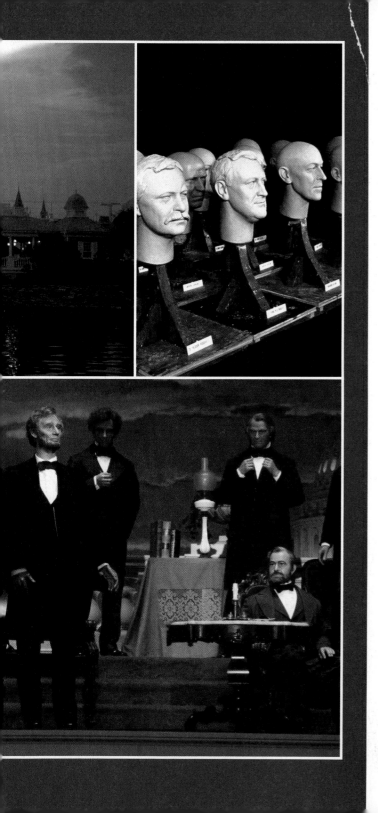

The Hall of Presidents

Liberty Square derives from two ideas originally intended for Disneyland—Edison Square, celebrating the American spirit of innovation, and Liberty Street, which would take visitors through Colonial America. Since the construction began for Walt Disney World only a short while before the United States celebrated its bicentennial, Liberty Square evolved into a perfect complement to the times. The Hall of Presidents, also an idea intended for Disneyland, artistically dramatizes the importance of America's role in the evolution of democracy. The marvels of space-age electronics are combined with the skills of Walt Disney Imagineering sculptors, artists, and dramatists to bring history "to life."

The show features an oration by Abraham Lincoln and concludes with a stirring portrayal of all our nation's presidents standing or seated on the stage, listening to an inspiring speech by the current commander-in-chief. The Audio-Animatronics programming involves the synchronization of movements—some as delicate as the twitch of an eye or the raising of an eyebrow—to narration and other "action" on the stage. To make the figures as accurate as possible, extensive and detailed research was conducted. All the costumes were meticulously handcrafted, using the sewing techniques and styles of cutting and stitching in vogue during each president's stay in office. The design teams studied documents, diaries, photographs, and, when available, films describing the personalities, mannerisms, and physical characteristics of each man. Each pair of glasses is the same prescription as the president who wore them, and upon close inspection, even the leg braces worn by Franklin Delano Roosevelt can be seen.

The attraction is housed in a white-trimmed, red-brick colonial hall designed to evoke the meeting houses of Boston and Philadelphia, where the young republic's most important documents—the Declaration of Independence and the Constitution of the United States—were forged. The date above the door, 1787, is the year the Constitution was ratified. The Great Seal located in the rotunda required an Act of Congress in order to be placed there. It is one of only three in the country (the others are in the White House Oval Office and at the Liberty Bell in Philadelphia).

The Haunted Mansion

Welcome, foolish mortals, to The Haunted Mansion, the only attraction featured in different lands at each of the first four Disney parks around the world. Its 999 grim, grinning, ghostly residents (but there's room for a thousand) are a potpourri of supernatural and historical types ranging from an Egyptian mummy, Great Caesar's ghost, medieval minstrels, and a headless knight, to a Valkyrie opera singer and a Victorian-era king and queen on a teeter-totter. But as you travel in your Doom Buggy, notice that you don't actually see any ghosts until Madame Leota calls out for them to join you during her séance scene. Fluttering bats, talking ravens, owls, cats, and baying hounds round out the mystical menagerie.

The exterior was changed from the antebellum mansion seen in Disneyland to a New York Hudson Valley Dutch-Gothic manor house more appropriate to its Liberty Square location. The names featured on the tombstones prior to the entrance are actually those of some of the Mansion's original designers and developers. The newest, and most animated, tombstone not only refers to Madame Leota, but also honors Imagineer Leota Thomas (née Toombs), who portrays the face in the séance room's crystal ball. She is also the form and voice of Little Leota at the end, encouraging visitors to make "final arrangements" to stay at the Mansion (they'll issue a "death certificate"). Periodically, the face on Leota's tombstone raises her chin and opens her eyes. The voice of the character in the crystal ball is that of Eleanor Audley, who also provided the voice for Maleficent in *Sleeping Beauty* and Lady Tremaine in *Cinderella*.

The five singing busts in the graveyard performing the signature song "Grim Grinning Ghosts" are the Mello Men, who include Thurl Ravenscroft (the broken bust on the left side), the original voice of Tony the Tiger. Contrary to the rumor, Walt Disney is not depicted on one of the singing statues.

Fantasyland

Cinderella Castle

With its conical towers and turrets, Cinderella Castle is the magical icon for Walt Disney World Resort. The base of the castle resembles a medieval fortress, typifying castles of the eleventh through thirteenth centuries, and the upper portion reflects the stately Gothic forms prominent in later centuries, symbolizing the evolution from fortress to Renaissance palace.

Thirteen gargoyles appear on the outside of the castle, and the inside passageway is decorated by a five-panel mosaic mural. Designed by Imagineer Dorothea Redmond, the mosaic contains hundreds of thousands of pieces of Italian glass in more than 500 colors, many of them fused with silver and 14-karat gold. In one scene, Cinderella tries on the slipper while her stepsisters look on. The stepsisters' cheek colors match their moods—Anastasia is flushed "red with rage" while Drizella is tinted "green with envy."

There are eighteen towers with corresponding spires outside the castle; the highest tower is gold in color. The remaining spires are blue, complementing the traditional gray, blue, and gold palette of the exterior, which is also graced by a coat of arms on the front and back of the castle that is of the Disney family. At Cinderella's Royal Table on the second floor, a bevy of princesses host an enchanting breakfast, followed by a royal lunch and dinner. If anyone asks you how many granite blocks were used to construct the castle, you can smartly answer "zero"—the castle is constructed from steel, cement, and fiberglass.

Cinderella's Golden Carrousel

Originally built by the Philadelphia Toboggan Company in 1917, Cinderella's Golden Carrousel features eighty-six horses—no two alike—that prance and romp beneath eighteen hand-painted scenes from *Cinderella*, basking in the glow of the carrousel's 2,325 lights. Each horse is numbered (underneath its bridle), and several have been given names, such as "King," the "lead" horse, dressed in ornate armor, and "Cindy," decorated with a gold ribbon on her tail (possibly Cinderella's horse itself!). There are five sizes of horses, arranged by the largest on the outside to the smallest on the inside in eighteen rows of five horses each.

The idea of having a carrousel was inspired by Walt Disney's frequent visits to Griffith Park in Los Angeles with his daughters. Watching his two young girls having fun while he sat on a park bench, Walt came up with the idea for an amusement park that an entire family could enjoy together.

What's the difference between a carrousel and a merry-go-round? Although the terms are frequently used interchangeably, some people define a carrousel as featuring only horses, while a merry-go-round can depict any beast or creature. Additionally, carrousels generally move counterclockwise and merry-go-rounds, or "roundabouts," move clockwise. Cinderella's Golden Carrousel once moved in a sideways motion. After it was initially set down during construction of the Park, Roy O. Disney noticed that, when viewed through the Castle entrance, the carrousel wasn't completely centered, and so it was re-installed for a better sight line.

Peter Pan's Flight

Inspired by the 1953 animated film, Peter Pan's Flight was originally conceived to have riders take the journey atop Peter's back as he flew over the rooftops of London. Though the concept was changed to the pirate galleons that now dip and soar from England to Never Land, passengers still enjoy the sensation of gliding through the evening skies as their vehicles are suspended from an overhead rail. Sharp eyes will notice dolls holding a tea party and Wendy reading to her brothers in an echo of the film's opening nursery scene as Tinker Bell zips past.

Dumbo the Flying Elephant

Standing on a hot air balloon and holding the "magic feather" that Dumbo believes will help him to fly, Timothy Q. Mouse watches over his protégé as sixteen large-eared, baby pachyderm–shaped vehicles soar through the skies of Fantasyland on this attraction based on the 1941 film. As pinwheels spin under the elephants' flights, a surrounding trio of elephant topiaries watches the fun.

Mickey's PhilharMagic

While the title of this amazing 3-D film may be *Mickey's PhilharMagic*, it's Donald Duck who takes center stage when he attempts to conduct the very *animated* instruments of the PhilharMagic Orchestra. Hitting a sour note from the start, Donald ends up flying in and out of scenes from various Disney films as he endeavors to retrieve Mickey's Sorcerer's Hat. The much-put-upon duck swims into part of Ariel's world (and loses his heart as well as some jewels), becomes the guest of Lumiere (viewers might want to "duck" themselves when the champagne bottles pop!), boogies with Simba, and takes a magic carpet ride beside Jasmine and Aladdin before contritely passing the baton back to Mickey.

Mickey's PhilharMagic features the largest seamless projection screen in the world, measuring 150 feet long and 28 feet high. With several of the animators associated with the original films involved in their character's development, this film represents the first time each featured Disney character was completely modeled and animated by computer. Donald's dialogue was created out of classic performances by the late Clarence "Ducky" Nash and supplemented by current quack-up voice actor Tony Anselmo.

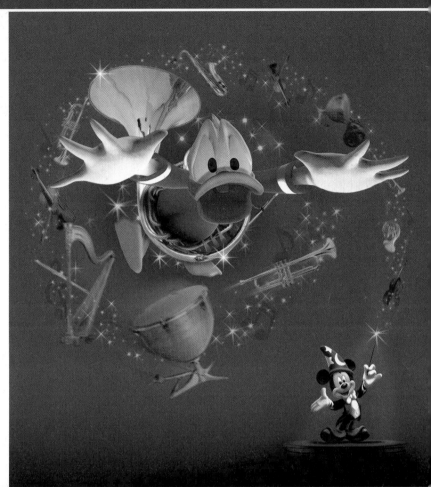

Snow White's Scary Adventures

Passengers ride inside "mine cars" named after the Seven Dwarfs as they follow the story of the fairest of them all as she escapes the wrath of the Magic Mirror–challenged evil Queen. Originally, Snow White wasn't even in the attraction, as the story was conceived to be shown from her point of view. A refurbishment in 1994 added the princess. When *Snow White and the Seven Dwarfs* debuted in 1937, it was the first full-length animated feature film, utilizing more than 750 artists over the course of three years. It received a special Academy Award in 1939 consisting of one full-size and seven miniature statuettes. Snow White's Scary Adventures and several other attractions at Fantasyland are known as "dark rides," since the action takes places inside, under minimal lighting. The scenery is painted with an ultraviolet technique that reveals subtle depths and details under various types of lighting, including UV and "theatrical lights."

Cinderella's Wishing Well

"La Fontaine de Cendrillon" is the name of the wishing well set across from Cinderella Castle courtyard, inspired by both a French fairy tale and the classic Walt Disney film. The fountain is more familiarly known as "Rags to Riches," as Cinderella

is portrayed in her patched dress and simple skirt. The "Riches" part? Subtly set in the decorative embellishments on the wall behind her is a crown that, when viewed from just the right angle (one that's about the right height for a young prince- or princess-in-the-making), seems to be set upon her head.

Belle's Storytime

As a book-reading heroine, Belle met a prince who wasn't so charming at first. *Beauty and the Beast* (1991) was the first animated film ever nominated for a Best Picture Academy Award, before becoming a magical Broadway musical. In the secluded outdoor stage at Fairytale Garden, Belle arrives reading (as usual). When she sees an audience of avid listeners, she asks if she can share her story, and invites lucky spectators to join her in the retelling.

Ariel's Grotto

Though Ariel stars in several attractions throughout Walt Disney World, this is the place to come face-to-fin with the red-haired princess. Surrounded by carved-out cave walls adorned with starfish, coral, and some under-the-sea treasures, Ariel greets her guests and poses for pictures. King Triton looks on from a pool nearby.

The Many Adventures of Winnie the Pooh

It's a blustery day in the Hundred-Acre Wood, as passengers in Hunny Pots are whisked through the pages of a giant storybook, encountering some very sweet adventures along the way. Travelers will see bubble-blowing Heffalumps and Woozles, bounce along with Tigger, and float through the floody place. In a tribute to the attraction formerly housed here—Mr. Toad's Wild Ride—a picture set on the left wall of Owl's house (one of the first scenes) depicts Toad handing over the deed to the property to Owl.

Mad Tea Party

If today is your "Unbirthday" (and the odds are 364 to 1 it is!), then it's time to take a spin at the silliest tea party in Wonderland. Based on the 1951 animated film *Alice in Wonderland*, eighteen spinning cups controlled by the passengers swirl and whirl on a giant tea tray underneath a canopy lit by Japanese tea lanterns. Perhaps the woozy dormouse who bobs up and down in the spinning center teapot has ridden it a few too many times? The topiaries at the entrance depict in leaves (not tea leaves, though) the Mad Hatter, March Hare, and Alice dancing on top of a long dining table bordered by two rather large chairs.

"it's a small world"

Originally created for the 1964–1965 New York World's Fair to benefit UNICEF, "it's a small world" moved to Disneyland in 1966, then was re-created on the East Coast to premiere in Walt Disney World at its opening. This musical extravaganza, hosted by "children" of the world, is populated by approximately 472 animated toys, props, and dolls, with each child wearing a symbolic costume. Walt conceived this attraction as a joyful singing and dancing tableau where nations are not defined, but where children from every area of the world are represented.

The attraction voyages through six major locations loosely grouped as Europe, Asia, Africa, Central and South America, The Islands, and The Finale, depicted with various architectural and geographical icons associated with each of the landmasses. The artistic flair of Imagineer Mary Blair is recognizable throughout; she used color to create different moods for each area. A variety of hues was used in the opening scenes through Europe; yellow represents the hot regions of the Middle East and Asia. Cool blues and greens were employed in Africa to create the impression of night, while warm yellows, oranges, and rusts color the fiesta scene for Mexico. Oranges and greens represent the lush rain forest theme for Central and South America, as purples and greens set a tropical tone for the Islands. The Finale glows with sky blues, silvers, and white—Blair's favorite color.

Composers Richard M. and Robert B. Sherman were commissioned by Walt to create a simple yet catchy tune that could be sung in several languages. Many native instruments are woven into the song's arrangement, including Scottish bagpipes, a Peruvian reed flute, and Tahitian drums. Mary Blair also designed the original signature facade, which finally made its way to Florida in a 2005 refurbishment. The space now comes to new life with the celebrated clockwork art in the interior queue area, whose face "rocks" to and fro as a gentle tick-tock and hourly musical chimes echo through the area.

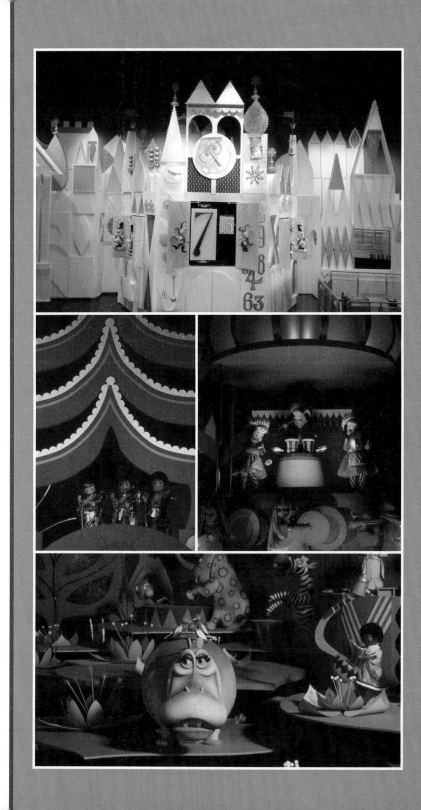

Mickey's Toontown Fair

Donald's Boat

The *Miss Daisy*, a cross between a tugboat and a leaky ocean liner, features Donald's distinctive color palette—the yellow of his bill, the blue of his uniform—and look—even the roof of the bridge resembles Donald's cap—as well as a twisted smokestack and a line bearing laundry, all surrounded by a foamy "duck pond" featuring lily pads that spout jumping streams and spray without warning. Young seafarers can blow the ship's whistle (watch out for a drenching!) or clang the boat's bell. Inside, a map drawn by Professor Ludwig Von Drake (Donald's uncle) of "Old Man and the Sea Enterprises" charts the Quack Sea, Mount Quackmore, and the way to sail into Toontown Fair.

The Barnstormer at Goofy's Wiseacres Farm

At Goofy's Wiseacres Farm, "squashed" squash, bell-shaped bell peppers, corn, tomatoes, and other plant life grow—in spite of the wayward way Goofy keeps his crops dusted. More than a few (chicken) feathers are ruffled when the Barnstormer, a "Multiflex Octoplane" based on a 1920s style bi-plane, soars around the farm before crashing through the hayloft of Goofy's classic red barn. Plane crazy, we'd call it. Goofy's two mail boxes are located in the most appropriate places—while one is posted in the ground, the second, for "Air Mail," is propped up by an airplane propeller.

Mickey's Country House

Set amongst clusters of candy-striped tents and fanciful fairground facades, this whimsical village is the place where you can visit your favorite Disney characters in their country getaway. Mickey's four-room craftsman-style mouse house is right in the heart of the Toontown fairgrounds. Inside, a radio in the living room is "tooned" to scores from Mickey's favorite football team—Duckburg University (versus Goofy Tech). In his den, Ping-Pong paddles shaped like Mickey, Donald, and Goofy's heads (Goofy's is next to the football trophy) await their next game.

Down the hall, Mickey's kitchen isn't quite ready to enter the Toontown Home Remodeling Contest—extreme decorators Donald and Goofy have left buckets of paint stacked in the sink, while the paint itself is spattered on the walls and floor. At least Mickey's bedroom closet is in order, with a crisp row of red long pants and tails at the ready. Hey, when you find a winning look, you should stick with it! Mickey keeps the rest of his wardrobe—over 175 different outfits—at the Studio. Just outside the kitchen, the garden features "Hollywooden vine" tomatoes, pumpkins, and cactus, all shaped in a familiar silhouette. If you don't find Mickey here, you can always catch him in his dressing room at the Judge's Tent to say hello and take a photo.

Minnie's Country House

In addition to being the editor of *Minnie's Country Cartoon Living Magazine*, Minnie's also an avid reader (note the copy of *Famous Mice in History* on her living room's coffee table), as well as a quilter, gardener, and blue ribbon–winning baker. Check out her Westingmouse fridge, which contains Golly Cheese Whiz, Cheese-Chip Ice Cream, and Philly Cheese Steaks. Her recipe for Cheesy Chocolate Chip cookies is posted on the door. There's popcorn in the microwave, and some Tasty Toon cake mix is set out on the counter as the cake itself rises quickly in her reliable Home on the Range stove. In the garden, a "palm" tree (made of hands, naturally!), feline-faced Tiger Lillies, and Twolips all bloom happily with Minnie's tender loving care.

Tomorrowland

Astro Orbiter

Tomorrowland was selected as the headquarters for the League of Planets, an interplanetary hub where sentient forms can meet. Here, robots perform household chores, ice cream comes from the Milky Way, and a trip through time is as convenient as a spin around the solar system. The "Future That Never Was" is finally here! At the center of the city, the Astro Orbiter glows with celestial neon colors that serve as a beacon to visitors, who can board machine-age rockets and take a spin through whirling planets. Originally called "Star Jets," there are similar versions of this attraction at all the Disney parks. At Disneyland, it's the Astro Orbitor (same route, different vowel).

Sonny Eclipse & Intergalactic Organ Show

Cosmic Ray's Starlight Café presents Sonny Eclipse, accompanied by his Space Angels, singing the "Planetary Boogie," among other hits. This stylin' lounge lizard, originally from Yew Nork City, on the planet Zork, is quite attached to the stage at the largest fast-food spot in Magic Kingdom Park.

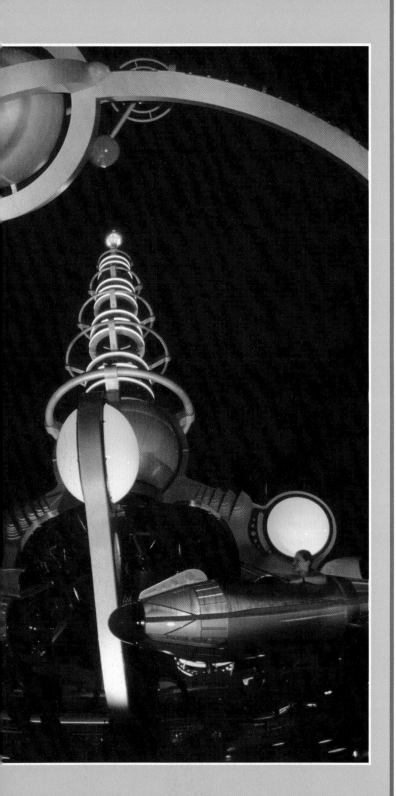

Monsters, Inc. Laugh Floor

There's nothing that can stop a one-eyed, green entrepreneur when he gets a good idea in his head (whichever part of him that is). Mike Wazowski, the hero from Disney•Pixar Animation Studio's feature *Monsters, Inc.*, has discovered that laughter is ten times more powerful than screams as a power source, so he's opened a comedy club for visiting humans that will generate power for the future of his hometown, Monstropolis. Management, represented by Roz, is not exactly sold on the idea, so Mike has a lot of pressure on him to make this scheme work. The Monsters, Inc. Laugh Floor is an immersive, interactive attraction in which the audience can laugh, joke, match wits, and laugh some more with comedian wannabes recruited by Monster-of-Ceremonies Mike.

Stitch's Great Escape!

After being greeted by Sergeant C4703BK2704-90210 at the Galactic Federation Prisoner Processing Center, new security recruits are inducted to help guard the common criminals sent through the facility. Experiment 626, a six-limbed blue alien who is a very *un*common criminal, attempts to outwit the galactic authorities even as two plasma cannons track this Level 3 prisoner's every move in the circular High Security Teleportation Chamber. Sights, sounds, and smells—chili dog, anyone?—add to the pandemonium. Will he escape? (We hope not.) Will he burp? (Loudly and quite odiferously.) Will he spit? (Definitely!)

The alien language seen throughout the Prisoner Teleport Center was inspired by designs created for the opening scenes of 2002's *Lilo & Stitch*. Graphic artists with Walt Disney Imagineering turned the designs into a practical alphabet that can be decoded into English. Many of the animators who worked on the movie partnered with Imagineers for the attraction, including director Chris Sanders, who provides the voice for Stitch again.

Stitch is one of the most complex Audio-Animatronics figures created to date—with more than 350 detailed, hand-machined parts, and more than forty separate functions—and he is also the first one to spit. (Ewwwwww!) The two plasma cannons that track Stitch's DNA each weigh more than 1,600 pounds. Recruits in the know will recognize a tenant of the previous attraction, The ExtraTERRORestrial Alien Encounter, in Skippy, the ever-hapless alien who has now been "volunteered" for a teleportation demonstration.

Buzz Lightyear's Space Ranger Spin

Where else in the universe can you join with Buzz Lightyear to fight evil forces to infinity and beyond? In this adventure, based on Disney•Pixar Animation Studios' feature *Toy Story 2*, Emperor Zurg is stealing Crystollic Fusion Power Units—C batteries to earthlings—and must be stopped as quickly as possible! Boarding an XP-37 Space Cruiser armed with infrared lasers, budding Space Rangers take a trip through the Astro Accelerator in order to travel from the Star Command Planet at the center of Gamma Quadrant to Planet Z in Sector 9. A lighted display inside the toy-spaceship vehicles helps keep score as sight and sound gags abound among the Z-shaped targets. Depending on your accuracy and prowess, your rank can fly from Space Cadet to Galactic Hero.

Space Mountain

In the early 1960s, Walt Disney and his Imagineers conceived the idea of a high-speed thrill attraction based on the excitement of the early Space Age. It would take more than ten years before the dream was realized, which happily allowed technology to catch up with Walt's vision.

Space Mountain was one of only four attractions that debuted at Walt Disney World prior to a similar attraction opening at Disneyland. Rising 180 feet above Magic Kingdom Park, Space Mountain's dramatic exterior is topped by spires that accentuate its "out of this world" appearance. Early plans had the attraction enclosed inside a dome, but Imagineer John Hench conceived a far more interesting version with "ribs" that would "reach for the sky" to help create the impression of height and the emphasis on soaring skyward. Basic construction techniques would have had the beams on the inside, but a flat surface was needed to project a filmed background of tumbling asteroids and luminous stars, so Hench "imagineered" the beams to be on the outside, giving the attraction a distinctive and effective modern design that differentiates it from all the other themed mountains in the parks. The mountain's cone-shaped structure contains 4,508,500 cubic feet of space—enough to hold a small skyscraper in its interior. Each one of the seventy-two pre-stressed concrete beams was hoisted into place by mammoth cranes.

Space Mountain was the first thrill attraction at Walt Disney World to be operated by a computer. It was also the first roller coaster of its kind to operate in perpetual darkness and was "flight-tested" before its opening by U.S. astronauts and Russian cosmonauts.

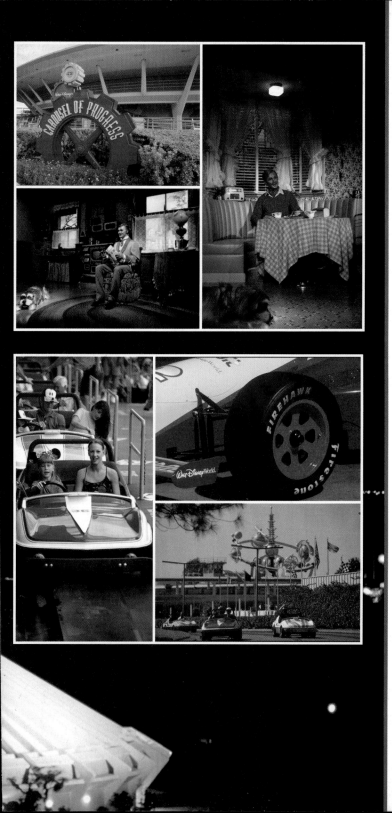

Walt Disney's Carousel of Progress

Walt Disney's Carousel of Progress musical-comedy show demonstrates the many conveniences made possible in American life by a century of technological innovation. Seated viewers get a glimpse into the homes of four generations of the same family, from the days before electricity to a sampling of what waits right around the corner. But here's the twist—it's the audience that moves and not the stage! An amazing technological development itself, the building's outer rim, where viewers sit in one of six 240-seat theaters, rotates around the core of six stationary stages where the show is presented.

The attraction was created for the 1964–1965 New York World's Fair, and featured the Sherman brothers' popular theme song, "There's a Great Big Beautiful Tomorrow." It was relocated to Disneyland in 1967, and ran there through 1973. The Walt Disney World version debuted in 1975, with a new exterior styling, a new scene added at the end, and a new song written by the Sherman brothers, "The Best Time of Your Life." During Tomorrowland's extensive renovation in 1994, the attraction was converted back to its original Disneyland 1960s look, and the original theme song was reinstated. Rover the dog has gone through as many variations as the attraction. His name changed several times, and his fur, which started out white, changed to light brown and is now dark brown.

Tomorrowland Indy Speedway

The Tomorrowland Indy Speedway, formerly named Grand Prix Raceway, moves by way of a linear induction motor—electromagnets move the cars around its 2,260-foot track without utilizing any onboard moving parts. Drivers wind through the banks and turns of the speedway while hearing the calls of a world-famous announcer from speakers positioned throughout the route. After finishing on one of its four lanes and arriving in Victory Circle, every driver gets a wave of the checkered flag.

SpectroMagic

Premiering on Walt Disney World's twentieth anniversary, the SpectroMagic Parade presents an amazing achievement of technology and imagination in a pageant of colors and characters that moves in concert with a soaring musical score.

SpectroMagic by the Numbers	
17	height in feet of Mickey's cape
24	length in feet of Mickey's cape from his shoulders to the base of his float
30	computers
38	feet of Chernabog's wingspan
46	characters from Disney films, not counting the Spectromen, butterflies and dragonflies, or bass fiddles
75	tons of lead/acid deep-cycle six volt-batteries needed to provide power
100	miles fiber-optic cable and threads
72,000	watts of light
250,000	fiber-optic points of lights
600,000	miniature bulbs
1 million	points of light, including costumes, floats, miniatures, and fiber optics

Wishes

"I bet a lot of you folks don't believe that—about a wish coming true," says narrator Jiminy Cricket. "The most fantastic magical things can happen—and it all starts with a wish!" In Wishes, the largest pyrotechnic display ever staged in Magic Kingdom Park, the power of a wish combines with magical music from Disney films and dazzling fireworks over and around Cinderella Castle. New pyrotechnics were created for the show, including a "blue star" that releases cascading sparkles, and an array of cometlike "wishing stars" that explode during the finale as the Blue Fairy reminds us to never stop believing in our wishes. Wishes can come true when we just believe in them with all our heart.